Magic Trix

The Witching Hour

Collect all the Magic Trix *books*

- ☑ The Witching Hour
- ☐ Flying High

The Witching Hour

Sara Grant

Illustrated by Erica-Jane Waters

Orion
Children's Books

First published in Great Britain in 2013
by Orion Children's Books
a division of the Orion Publishing Group Ltd
Orion House
5 Upper St Martin's Lane
London WC2H 9EA
An Hachette UK company

1 3 5 7 9 10 8 6 4 2

The Orion Publishing Group's policy is to use papers
that are natural, renewable and recyclable products and
made from wood grown in sustainable forests. The logging
and manufacturing processes are expected to conform to the
environmental regulations of the country of origin.

A catalogue record for this book is
available from the British Library.

ISBN 978 1 4440 0777 0

Printed in Great Britain by Clays Ltd, St Ives plc

To my lovely editor Amber Caravéo for
inspiring the series and adding the sparkle
to *Magic Trix*!

Chapter One

The long black tail swished from side to side with each *tick tock*. The yellow googly eyes looked left then right. The big and little hands clicked into position, both pointing straight up. Trixibelle's black cat clock meowed twelve times.

It was midnight. Trix's birthday was officially over. She was ten years and one day old. Double digits. That was nearly a teenager. Like every year, she'd asked for a kitten. She squeezed her eyes shut and wished and hoped and prayed one last time. She crossed her fingers and toes and even whispered "Abracadabra" for extra luck.

When she opened her eyes, she saw lots and lots of cats – on her pyjamas, her duvet and the posters hanging on her wall. She had a collection of twenty-three toy cats scattered around her room, but none of them was real. Her dad was allergic to cats so her wish was never ever going to come true.

Trix wriggled out of bed. She batted the ten balloons that her parents had tied onto her bedpost that morning. Nine balloons floated above her and one sad, wrinkly red balloon flopped on her pillow. Her stupid little brother Oscar had popped it and also scribbled out the second 'ir' in the *Birthday Girl* sign that hung on her door and replaced it with 'hou' so the message now read *Birthday Ghoul*.

She took a huge bite of the slice of birthday cake she'd sneaked up to her room. Chocolate cake. With double-chocolate icing and chocolate sprinkles on top! If she were a cat, she would be purring. Chocolate always made her feel that way. Chocolate and birthdays and kittens!

Trix stared out at the full moon high in the sky over her best friend Holly's house. The moon glistened like a million twinkle lights. Trix loved full moons because her Aunt Belle had told her they were magical.

Suddenly, Trix spotted something out of the corner of her eye – a shadow zipping through the night sky, heading straight for her big beautiful moon. What was it? She squinted to get a better look. A strange outline came into focus.

Could it be . . . ?

Trix rubbed her eyes. She must be dreaming.

Pointy hat.

Broomstick.

And, was that . . .

Yes, a cat was perched on the bushy end of a broom!

Trix couldn't believe her eyes – a real live witch!

Trix pointed her torch out of the window
and flicked it on and off three times really
fast. The light bounced off the four mirrors
attached to branches high in the tree between
Trix and Holly's houses. The mirrors were
positioned so that light from Trix's torch
would flash right onto Holly's pillow. Trix
and Holly had rigged up this emergency
message system themselves.

Trix watched as the witch soared through
the sky. She was pretty sure this wasn't a

dream. She flashed the torchlight again, but Holly's window remained dark.

Now was the time for action! Trix shuffled into her mismatched slippers – one pink and one green. She pulled on her green polka-dot dressing gown and dashed out of her room. She jumped down the stairs two at a time and skidded to a stop, barely avoiding a collision with Oscar.

"Hey!" Oscar shouted, a little too loudly for midnight.

"Hey, yourself." Trix paused for a second when she spotted a piece of *her* birthday cake in his hand. "That's my cake," Trix said, swiping a fingerful of icing.

Oscar shoved the rest of the cake in his mouth. "What are you doing up?" he asked, showering Trix with chocolate bits as he spoke.

"Mind your own business," Trix said and pushed past him.

Outside in her front garden, Trix waved wildly as the witch zoomed across the moon.

"Holly!" Trix whisper-shouted at Holly's window. "Wake up or you're going to miss the most amazing thing ever."

The witch loopity-looped and waved to Trix before disappearing into a cloud. The tingles in Trix's tummy erupted into full fizzy fireworks. Trix twirled with her arms stretched out wide, unable to contain her excitement.

Holly's window creaked open. "Huh? Wha—? W-what's the m-matter?" Holly stammered as she rubbed sleep from her eyes. Trix stifled a laugh. Her best friend's normally perfectly styled hair seemed to have exploded. Red springy curls jetted from her head like sunbeams.

"I just saw a witch," Trix told Holly.

"Weirdo!" Oscar's voice made Trix jump. He was standing at the front door of their house, his mouth still ringed with chocolate from *her* birthday cake. "You probably just saw your reflection in the mirror," he added, and stuck out his tongue.

"Trixibelle Elizabeth Morgan!" came a voice from behind her. It was her mum. All Trix's tingly excitement was snuffed out like birthday-cake candles after the first big blow. Mum used her full name when she was in big-ish trouble. Trix loved her name. She only knew one other person with the same name – her very favourite aunt. But Aunt Belle used the last bit as her nickname while Trix used the first.

"Oscar, get inside," Mum said. "Good night, Holly." She waved goodbye to Trix's friend.

Sorry, Holly mouthed as she closed her curtains.

"Little girls should not be outside by themselves at this time of night," Mum said as she ushered Trix back towards the house.

"I'm not a little girl any more, remember? I'm ten," Trix said and dragged her heels so she could glance at the sky one last time. The full moon still shimmered in the inky blackness, but the witch had vanished.

"OK, *big* girls should not be out at this time of night." Mum placed a kiss on the top of Trix's head.

"But I saw . . ." Trix wanted to tell Mum, but she couldn't. No one but Holly would ever believe her. "Never mind."

As Mum tucked her into bed, Trix closed her eyes and held the image of the witch in her mind. She wanted to stick it in her memory for ever, like the gold star she'd got on her spelling test. But the image gradually faded into the rainbow swirl of dreams.

Chapter Two

At school the next morning, lack of sleep made Trix's head feel as if it were stuffed with marshmallows. She and Holly hurried into the school hall and took their seats near the front like they did every Monday for assembly.

"Did you really see a . . ." Holly paused, looked from side to side to make sure no one was listening and then spelled in her super quietest voice, "W.I.T.C.H.?"

Trix shrugged. She felt sort of silly about the whole thing now. Ten years old was *too* old to believe in things like witches. Maybe it had been a hallucination caused by eating chocolate at midnight.

"I bet you *did*," Holly went on. "If there were going to be witches anywhere in the world, I'm sure they'd live here in Little Witching."

"I suppose," Trix muttered.

"Or maybe only miniature witches live in *Little* Witching." Holly snort-laughed at her own joke. "What does a little witch make?"

"I don't know," Trix replied.

"Mini-magic." Holly nudged Trix with her elbow. "Get it? Mini-magic."

Trix couldn't help but laugh. The joke wasn't that funny, but Holly's giggle-snort of laughter always made her smile.

Holly dug around in the pocket of her midnight blue Little Witching uniform. "I've been practising. Watch this." She held up a pound coin.

Holly pinched the coin between her thumb and index finger. "I will make this coin disappear." She looked around to make sure no one was watching. Then she cupped her other hand over the coin. "Abracadabra!" She swept her hands apart. "Ta da!"

Plink! Plink!

Holly's face flushed pink as the coin bounced on the tile floor.

"You almost had it that time," Trix said, scooping up the coin.

"There is no 'almost' for great magicians." Holly sighed and took the coin from Trix.

"Maybe you need a new magic word," Trix suggested. "Allicabizzle or Dabracabra."

"Yeah, maybe."

"I know you'll be a great magician some day." Trix smiled at her best friend. "Then you can make Oscar the Horrible disappear."

"That will be my mission in magic," Holly said. "What did he do this time?"

"He ate the last piece of my birthday cake *and* turned my favourite necklace into a fishing lure."

"Not the feathery green one I gave you on our first sleepover-versary?" Holly asked, eyes wide with horror. Trix and Holly celebrated everything – from when they'd learned to tie their shoes, to the first time they'd been allowed to walk to school by themselves, to last week when they'd both spilled orange-mango squash on their school uniforms.

Trix nodded. "The necklace is now covered in pond goo."

"Yuk!" Holly shivered. "For my next trick, I will turn Oscar the Horrible into a frog so he can live with all the other slimy creatures in your pond." Holly pointed an imaginary wand at Oscar as he scuttled by with his Year Two class.

"Ladies and gentlemen of Little Witching Primary School," the headmistress called as she marched down the centre aisle. "May I have your attention please?" Trix was sure Miss Abernathy could quiet a zoo full of roaring lions with those simple words. She stood at the front of the hall and called the morning assembly to order. "Today we will start a new programme with the Enchanted Grove School for Girls."

The quiet from moments ago was swallowed

by a mumble of disappointment. Trix and Holly groaned.

"This is worse than Brussels sprouts," Trix told Holly.

"Brussels sprouts covered in Marmite and buried in my dad's stinky socks," Holly replied. "Those girls are not very friendly. They never, ever speak to us – not at the bus stop or on the High Street."

I suppose we never speak to them either, Trix thought.

"Quieten down," Miss Abernathy continued. "From now on, the Enchanted Grove School for Girls will spend their last class with us every day. Isn't that lovely? This is a great opportunity to make new friends." She waved several sheets of paper in the air. "You get to pick a brand new extraordinary class to attend. The sign-up sheets for all available options will be posted on the school noticeboard. You can sign up after assembly. There are only a limited number of places so if your first choice is full, please try something new. You never know when magic will strike!" She loved to say that. It was practically the school motto.

"You could say the same about lightning," Holly whispered to Trix, "and that can kill you!" The girls burst into laughter.

After assembly, Trix rushed to the noticeboard. She was determined to sign up for the best activity. No chess or wood-working for her or, worse yet, school subjects the teachers tried to dress up as fun, like maths magicians or history heroes. *Yuk!* Trix slipped through gaps in the crowd until she was standing in front of the board.

She looked at the titles of the sign-up sheets. "Stupid. Boring. No. Never. Not a chance. I'd rather spend time with my brother," she muttered as she read.

The spaces were filling up as her classmates scribbled down their names. Trix could feel time running out and it made her insides jumpy. *There's got to be something not horrible*, she thought. She was being jostled like a jingle ball in a pile of kittens.

Then at the farthest corner of the noticeboard, she spotted a nearly blank sheet. The word *Witchcraft* was written at the top of the page. Trix's stomach hiccupped. That was the one! She quickly signed her name – and Holly's. Then she stood on tiptoe and searched for her best friend.

"Holly, over here!" Trix called.

Everyone instantly stopped and stared at Trix and Holly. Holly turned as red as a lobster eating a tomato swimming in an ocean of ketchup. Trix wished everyone could see how funny and smart and all-around amazing her friend was, but that was never going to happen when the only person Holly ever spoke to was Trix.

Trix pulled Holly away from the crowd. "You're never going to believe it. I've signed us up for the most perfect thing ever."

"What?" Holly asked, bouncing up and down, already excited.

"Our new activity is . . ." Trix paused like those talent-show judges on the TV.

"Tell me!" Holly nearly shouted, and blushed when a few heads turned.

Trix leaned in and whispered in Holly's ear, "Witchcraft."

"Really?" A smile lit up Holly's face. Trix grinned in response.

"All right, my little witchings," Miss Abernathy sing-songed, "time for lessons. If you haven't chosen a new class, one will be selected for you." She placed her hand on Trix's shoulder and gently guided her towards

Year Five's classroom. "How lovely that you and Holly signed up for Arts and Crafts in the library."

What?

Trix twisted so she could get one last look at the noticeboard. *That can't be right*, she thought. But the sheet, which moments ago she was sure had been entitled *Witchcraft*, now had the words *Arts and Crafts* printed neatly at the top of the page. Trix's heart sank. Maybe she had witches on the brain after her midnight sighting, but it was going to take more than magic to make this mistake up to Holly.

Chapter Three

When the bell rang signalling time for the last class of the day, Trix and Holly took the long way round to the library. They were in no hurry to start Arts and Crafts. Trix imagined having to recycle plastic bottles and cardboard boxes into some stupid work of modern art. Holly sighed loudly.

"It won't be so bad," Trix said as they climbed the stairs that led to the library. "At least we'll be together." She stopped dead in her tracks when she saw a pink and purple flash disappear into the library.

"Was that . . ." Holly began.

Trix nodded. It was the pink and purple of the Enchanted Grove School for Girls uniform. Trix and Holly ducked out of sight and watched as two more pink and purple figures slipped through the heavy wooden library doors. Trix's hopes for an un-horrible afternoon vanished.

"An afternoon with Enchanted Grove girls. Not so bad, huh?" Holly asked, backing down the stairs. "I'd rather eat a bowl of rotten aubergines covered in slug slime."

"Yuk!" Trix laughed in spite of the gooey feeling of dread oozing through her veins. "We might as well get it over with." Trix charged through the library doors before she could change her mind.

The library was empty, except for Lulu the librarian who always insisted the pupils call her by her first name, and who was currently hunched behind a pile of books.

"Welcome, my lovelies!" Lulu pushed her cat's-eye shaped glasses up the bridge of her nose. Lulu always looked like a puzzle made with pieces from different pictures. Her skirt was dotted with blue flowers. Her shirt was yellow and checked and her waistcoat was sunshine orange.

Lulu's silvery-white hair was twisted into a messy bun and secured with pencils and paperclips. Today it stuck out like a lopsided teacake on the top of her head. One lone curl spiralled down the side of her face. She twisted it around and around her finger as she spoke. "Oh, Holly, I'm so terribly sorry but too many girls have signed up for Arts and Crafts."

Trix looked around the empty room. "But—" she started.

Lulu raised her hand, which set the bangles on her wrist jangling. "Let me finish. Holly, you have been reassigned to Cookery in the kitchen. They are making biscuits today. That should be fun. Now, run along."

Holly hugged Trix goodbye and then shuffled out of the library.

"Sometimes bad turns out to be better," Lulu said and winked at Trix.

But Trix was a million per cent sure this was definitely worse.

"You are in for a real treat." Lulu stood and spun on her tippy toes. With Lulu's eye-watering wardrobe, it was like watching a rainbow in a blender. "We are going to start with a brief history of Ancient Egyptian Pottery." She stopped spinning.

Creeping cats! Trix thought. *History and pottery in the same sentence can't be good.*

"Please go to the last bookcase at the very back of the library and bring me the biggest book."

Trix's eyebrows scrunched together in confusion.

"Never waste time unless you can make it," Lulu said and gave Trix a gentle push in the right direction.

Trix didn't want to go back there. No one ever went back there. That was where all the super-boring books were kept. Trix dragged her feet but eventually reached the last bookcase at the very back of the library. Cobwebs decorated every corner. The lights flickered.

Trix brushed her fingers along the spines looking for Lulu's book. She coughed at the dust cloud she created. There it was. It had the silhouette of a cat on the spine and it was glowing.

But that was impossible!

As Trix reached for the book, the bookcase transformed before her eyes. Trix blinked and blinked again. The bookcase was now an

ancient-looking door, which creaked ajar.

Part of Trix wanted to run, but another part – the part that made her peek at scary movies and shake her Christmas presents – wanted to stay. A secret room was hidden behind the last bookcase in the library of Little Witching Primary School. Trix stepped inside.

Chapter Four

As she walked through the door, Trix's excitement bubbled up like the green goo boiling in the cauldron in the middle of the room.

Cauldron?

But that wasn't the weirdest thing.

Trix opened her eyes as wide as they would go. She couldn't believe what she was seeing. Lulu was standing in front of her. At least

Trix thought it was Lulu. She had Lulu's white hair, but instead of being tied up in a bun, silvery curls flowed down her back. Her wrists were still covered with bangles, but her glasses were gone and she was now dressed in a beautiful black gown like a film star might wear to a haunted house. On top of her head was a pointy black hat, just like the one the witch had been wearing last night when she flew across the moon.

But even that wasn't the weirdest thing.

"Trix, join us!" Lulu said, waving at Trix to gather round with three Enchanted Grove pupils and another girl called Becka who was from Trix's class. "Each of you girls has the gift of magic," Lulu told them. "I am pleased to officially welcome you as witches into the Sisterhood of Magic!"

Yep, *that* was the weirdest thing. Lulu, who wasn't *just* a librarian any more, was telling Trix, who *was* just a girl, that she was actually a witch!

Trix wondered if her brain was playing tricks on her again. Crazy, silly thoughts did sometimes pop into her head – such as, what if the funny blinking toad in the pond in her back garden really was a prince? She hadn't tried to kiss it, though she might have if she could have caught it. Her brain liked to imagine things that couldn't possibly be true. This must be one of those times because Lulu the librarian couldn't possibly have said that she, Trixibelle Morgan, was a witch!

"Witches become magical when they

turn double-digits," Lulu said. "You have all recently turned ten years old." Her eyes sparkled as if they were caught in camera flashes. "And each of you saw something strange last night at midnight – the witching hour – didn't you?"

Trix nodded. How did Lulu know?

"Only real witches can see another witch's midnight ride," Lulu explained. "On our broomstick flights, witches are invisible to everyone else."

"That was you last night?" Trix blurted, then she clapped her hands over her mouth. She hadn't meant to say it out loud.

"Me – and Sparkles, my cat." Lulu smiled. "Little Witching is secretly the world headquarters for the Sisterhood of Magic. This society can be traced all the way back to Cinderella's fairy godmother."

Lulu must have seen the confused looks on the girls' faces because she paused to let that idea soak in. "I have been appointed by the Sisterhood to teach you about the wonderful world of magic. With this new gift comes great responsibility. Witches must use their magical abilities to help others. We will train together every school day. Your magic will continue to grow, and I will show you how to control and use your new skills for good."

Trix's brain was turning somersaults. She couldn't be a witch, could she? Surely witches must *know* they are witches, and Trix usually felt the opposite of magical. On her birthday, Christmas, the start of the summer holidays and when she ate chocolate, Trix felt the *tiniest* bit magical, but other than that Trix's life was plain and ordinary.

"And the best and the brightest of you will one day become fairy godmothers." Lulu looked at each girl. "It's the highest honour that can be bestowed upon a witch."

Before Lulu could say another word, one of the Enchanted Grove girls stepped forwards. She flipped her perfectly straightened blonde hair over her shoulder and cleared her throat. "My name is Stella Arabella Alexandra Ferguson and these are my best friends, Pippa and Cara." She pointed to the two other Enchanted Grove girls. Both also had blonde hair, one in a low and the other in a high ponytail. Trix couldn't tell which was which but she recognised all three friends. They were usually waiting at the bus stop in the morning when Trix and Holly walked to school. "And this is my new friend, Becka." Stella nodded towards the only other girl from Little Witching. She had brown hair in a fancy long plait. "We're friends even though she goes to Little Witching."

"Th—" Lulu started, but Stella raised her hand.

"Um, I wasn't quite finished, miss." Stella stood up a bit straighter and continued, "This comes as no surprise to me, Miss Lulu."

Now Lulu interrupted. "It's just Lulu."

"As I was saying, some of you may be surprised to learn you are a witch," Stella said. Trix couldn't be sure but it seemed that Stella looked right at her when she said that.

"But I come from a long line of witches. My mum and granny are witches too and they have already taught me a few tricks."

Stella faced her friends. *"Sparkle, glitter, shimmer, shine. Give my friends a gift that's fine."* Stella pointed to Pippa, Cara and Becka's throats and a glimmer of light shot from her fingertip, leaving a tiny cluster of gems on a sparkling chain around each girl's neck.

Trix rubbed her naked throat, remembering how her brother had ruined her favourite necklace. She felt a pang of jealousy as she looked at the other girls' beautiful new jewellery and thought about Stella's magical ability.

"Thank you, Stella," Lulu said, turning so only Trix could see her and rolling her eyes a little. That made Trix feel a smidge better. "Your turn to introduce yourself," Lulu said and nodded to Trix.

"My name is Trixibelle Morgan." An army of butterflies seemed to invade her tummy. "But everyone calls me Trix."

"What kind of a name is that?" Trix heard Stella whisper to her friends, who giggled.

Trix ignored Stella and continued, "I don't think there are any witches in my family, but then again, I didn't think there were any witches in my school."

Lulu put a reassuring hand on Trix's shoulder. "I know this is a lot to take in. But you are all witches, I promise you," she said. "I will teach you all about spells and potions, and you'll learn how to ride on your very own broomstick. It takes time, patience and practice to master the art of witchcraft."

Trix laughed to herself. In a way she *was* going to learn about arts and crafts – the art of magic and the craft of being a witch.

Lulu strolled over to a bookcase that was jammed with bottles and jars. Some glowed, while others had squiggly, squirmy things inside. There were powders and liquids of every colour. "The first thing any young witch needs is a familiar," Lulu said.

Pippa raised her hand. "What's a familiar?" Her ponytail swished back and forth when she spoke.

"A familiar is a magical spirit that usually takes the form of an animal and helps its witchy companion with her magic," Lulu explained. "Think of your familiar as your very own enchanted pet."

Lulu's black flowy skirt swished at her ankles as she danced around the room, selecting a pinch of this and a dash of that. She tossed all the ingredients into the cauldron, which was as big as Mum's washing machine, and began to chant:

"I call upon the spirits
of magic and of nature.
Please send a menagerie
of magical creatures."

Trix held her breath as a purplish smoke bubbled from the cauldron and spilled into the room. The air cooled and was filled with the strangest sounds. Trix heard barking and mewing and chirping and grunting and howling and snapping and tweeting. When the smoke cleared, the secret room in the library of Little Witching Primary School looked more like a zoo than a classroom.

Trix recognised most of the animals, even if they had different colours and patterns from usual. There was a yellow toad, a little orange elephant with wings, a lavender rat, and a snow-white owl that was turning its head around and around. Trix loved all the unique creatures, but she knew immediately which one would be her familiar. Batting at the tail of a twinkling pink bunny was a cute black kitten with white spots. Or was it a white kitten with black spots? It didn't matter. She and that kitten were meant to be together. Trix knew it in her heart.

Trix sidestepped a duck-billed platypus and tiptoed between a pug and a rainbow-striped bird. She had almost reached the kitten when the most awful thing happened.

Stella Arabella Alexandra Ferguson swooped in and scooped up the little cat. "This adorable kitten simply *must* be my familiar!" she declared.

A moment ago Trix's heart had felt light and fluffy like candyfloss, but now it felt as though it were covered in sticky, bitter marmalade. Horrible Stella had stolen her kitten!

Chapter Five

This girl smells like roses and I don't like roses, Jinx the kitten thought. Roses are too rosy. He felt as if he were drowning in a puddle of petals. He wiggled his body from the top of his pink nose to the tip of his black tail. The pink, fluffy girl was not the witch for him. He leaped from her arms with a twist.

"Witches do not pick their familiars," Lulu said. "It's the other way around."

Jinx flicked his tail in agreement. He liked Lulu. Lulu was like sunshine and bumble-bees all mixed together.

Jinx hopped and skipped from one girl to the next. Oh, there was so much to think about. The right witch had to be kind and funny. She would let him sleep in her bed, and she needed to know how to scratch the right place behind his ear.

Jinx's paws kept tripping each other up. He tumbled and rolled and picked himself up again.

Too dirty, he thought. He sat and licked a white spot and then a black one, enjoying the tug of his rough tongue across his fur. He needed to look his best when he picked his very own witch.

Oops, Lulu was speaking again, Jinx realised. What was she saying? What had he missed?

Lulu waved her arms in the air as if she were conducting an orchestra. Her bracelets jingled and jangled. "Another magical moment! Familiars, please select your witches."

Jinx's ears tingled and his little heart thumped with excitement. The white owl fluttered over to Becka. The tabby cat picked Cara. Pippa looked rather sad when the lavender rat sniffled over to her. Even the rosy girl had a familiar— a pug who called himself Rascal.

The girl named Trix took a step back from the circle. No familiar had picked her yet. There was something about her that was different from the rest of the girls. Looking at her made Jinx's tummy feel funny. It was the way he felt when he saw a colourful butterfly or sniffed a beautiful flower.

"Jinx Jingle Jangle," Lulu called.

Jinx's ears pricked up at the sound of his own marvellously magical name. He scampered over to Lulu and rubbed against her legs.

"Jinx, my darling kitty, you need to choose. Or have you decided you don't want to be a familiar?" Lulu asked and gave him a little stroke.

Jinx wanted to be a familiar. He wanted it more than anything. He stretched his neck and nodded his chin.

"Go on then," Lulu said and nudged him forwards.

Jinx crouched down and flicked his tail from side to side. Then he dashed straight to the girl he felt in his twitching whiskers was the right witch for him. He leaped right into Trix's arms and snuggled in the crook of her neck. She smelled of chocolate. Jinx purred and Trix laughed. They were a perfect match. Jinx could feel his spots sparkle – that's what they always did when he was happy.

Chapter Six

Trix cuddled the beautiful sparkling kitten. She couldn't imagine feeling happier than she did at this moment. She had her very own kitten at last.

"Magic up, my little witches," Lulu said and clapped her hands.

Trix and the other girls formed a circle around Lulu. Jinx blinked his golden eyes at Trix.

"You and your familiar will be working together for a long time. When the bond between a familiar and a witch is strong, the familiar can help its witch perform more powerful spells. They can also protect you when your magic is new and you are learning how to use it." Lulu inspected every partnership as she spoke. She rubbed the lavender rat's ears, smoothed the white owl's feathers, stroked the tabby cat, and touched noses with the pug. "Your familiar will be your connection to the witching world, bringing messages from the Sisterhood of Magic. Your first assignment is to get to know your familiar. As your magic improves so will your bond with your familiar. They aren't like ordinary pets. They can take care of themselves. They will never be far away from you, but they may be absent from time to time if they are needed by the Sisterhood of Magic."

Trix snuggled Jinx closer. She could hear and feel Jinx purring. They were going to be great friends, Trix just knew it.

"Now for introductions!" Lulu said.

Pippa raised her hand. "But, miss, we've already done that," she said with a confused swish of her ponytail.

Lulu took a deep breath. "I meant I'll introduce your familiars."

"Oh . . ." Pippa's cheeks turned the same shade as her Enchanted Grove school uniform. *Even her blushes are colour coordinated*, Trix thought.

"You've all met Jinx," Lulu said and winked at Trix and Jinx. "Pippa, I would like to introduce you to Duchess Violet Von Twitch," Lulu said with a sweeping bow.

"Where?" Pippa's ponytail whipped from side to side as she looked around. "I'd like to meet a duchess."

"I think she means the rat," Trix said, curtseying to the rat like her Aunt Belle had taught her in case she ever met the Queen.

The lavender rat was standing on her hind legs and appeared to be waving to an imaginary crowd.

Pippa knelt down and shook the rat's tiny paw. "Oh, hello, Duchess . . ." Pippa squinted up at Lulu. "What was her name again?"

"Everyone calls her Twitch," Lulu said and moved on to the tabby cat. "Cara, I see you've already met Princess Tabitha."

The girl who had a low ponytail was on her hands and knees. She had untied the ribbon from her hair and tied it around the cat's neck in a pretty bow. "She likes to be called Tabby," Cara said and Tabby nodded.

Lulu walked over to Becka, who had a white owl perched on her shoulder. "And this show-off," Lulu said as the owl turned his

head almost all the way round, "is Sherlock Nocturne. Sherlock is a wise old bird. You are very lucky to have him, Becka."

"Thank you, miss," Becka said and turned so she and Sherlock were nose to beak. "Pleasure to meet you."

Sherlock hooted his response.

Stella was sitting cross-legged with her arms folded high across her chest while a pug ran in circles around her.

"And this is Rascal," Lulu said, giving the pug a treat from a pocket hidden in her flowing black skirt.

"Doesn't he have some fancy name?" Stella frowned.

Lulu's lips formed a tight red line before she answered. "Yes, but his proper name is ancient Chinese and quite unpronounceable."

"Sparkle, glitter, shimmer, shine," Stella said. *"Make this pup look more like mine."* With a *poof* and a flash of pink, Rascal was transformed into a Chihuahua with a pink bow on his head and a collar that matched Stella's school uniform. "That's more like it," Stella said and cradled the dog in her arms. Rascal squirmed and whined until Stella set him free.

"I need your listening ears." Lulu clapped to get everyone's attention. "The first rule of the Sisterhood of Magic is that no one must know you are a witch," Lulu said in her most serious voice. "Also," Lulu glared at Stella, "you are not allowed to perform any magic that I have not specifically taught you in class." Lulu swirled her finger over Rascal's head. With a *whoosh* and a shower of glitter, Rascal was once again an ordinary pug. He barked and wagged his curly tail.

"It has been a magical first meeting," Lulu said. "I will see you all tomorrow!"

Trix couldn't believe it was time to go. She gently bumped heads with Jinx. She wasn't ready to leave her new familiar already.

"Magic marbles, I almost forgot!" Lulu exclaimed. She said a magic spell and then clicked her fingers five times. Now each girl was holding a lopsided clay pot. Trix's was the shade of daffodils and leaned to the right. She thought it looked beautifully silly, just like something she would make. "As far as anyone knows, these are what we made in Arts and Crafts today."

"Couldn't you have at least made them a bit prettier?" Stella muttered and her friends giggled.

"Beauty finds the beautiful," Lulu said and shared a secret smile with Trix. Stella looked confused but Trix thought she understood what Lulu meant. "Tootles, my little witches.

Have a magical time until we meet again."
The secret door to the library creaked open.

Twitch scampered inside Pippa's huge pink
handbag. Sherlock shrank to thumb size and
nestled into Becka's plait. He now looked
like a feathery hair clip. Tabby and Rascal
tumbled alongside Cara and Stella.

As Stella slipped out from behind the
bookcase, Trix heard her whisper a rhyme
and Stella's wonky vase became a perfect pink
teacup. Stella noticed Trix staring and gave a
smug shrug.

"What's the matter, Trix?" Lulu said when
she realised Trix hadn't left.

"I love Jinx," Trix said, kissing the kitten
between his pointy ears. "But I can't take him
home. I'm not allowed a pet." The thought of
leaving Jinx made Trix want to cry.

"I'm not a witch for nothing. My brain
needs a moment to be magical." Lulu
squeezed her eyes shut tightly and appeared
to be thinking really, really hard.

Suddenly, a shower of sparkles burst from
Lulu's head and her eyelids popped open.

"That's it! I've got an idea."

Lulu studied the shelves filled with jars and bottles. She grabbed a dash of this and a pinch of that and placed all the ingredients in a bowl. As she stirred the mixture, her whole body began to blur. "This should do it." She handed the bowl to Trix. "Sprinkle this over Jinx and repeat after me."

Jinx leaped from Trix's arms and landed at her feet. He sat up straight and tall as if he were waiting for what came next.

Trix scooped up the mixture in her hand. It was cool and hot all at the same time.

"*I clal puno het tisserohod rof noe staglin pells,*" Lulu said the strange words, and Trix did her best to repeat them. "*Os Jinx nac chawt rove Trix, sleepa kema mih slibvie ot siwtech lyno.*"

Trix repeated the spell but it made no sense.

"Advanced magic," Lulu explained.

Trix sprinkled the mixture over Jinx. He shook from the tip of his nose to the tip of his tail and then rolled on the ground in delight. He began to glow and then – *poof!* – Jinx was gone. Trix's excitement melted away like chocolate fudge ripple ice cream in the summer sun.

"This potion and spell will make Jinx invisible in the real world. Witches will still see him but no one else can." Lulu smiled. "Problem solved."

Jinx's spots sparkled and Trix could see his ghostly outline.

"Thanks, Lulu!" Trix grinned and gave Lulu the biggest hug ever. "Come on, Jinx. Let's go home."

Trix felt all glittery inside.

Chapter Seven

"I can't wait for you to meet Holly," Trix told Jinx as they left for school the next morning. "She's going to love you."

Jinx bounded into the front garden, but Trix stopped in her tracks. Holly wasn't going to be able to see Jinx. And Trix couldn't tell her best friend about her mighty magical afternoon because that would break the first rule of the Sisterhood of Magic. She had never kept a secret from Holly before. OK, she'd kept special presents a surprise at birthdays and Christmas. But she told Holly everything else – even when she'd borrowed Holly's favourite blue, glittery designer T-shirt and spilled fruit punch on it. She'd been tempted to blame Oscar, but she'd told Holly the truth and Holly had forgiven her. That's what best friends did.

Jinx weaved among the flowers that lined Trix's front garden, making them sway as if they were dancing. He nudged a rainbow-coloured rubber ball that Oscar had left outside. He tumbled and rolled, and Trix laughed as the kitten's spots sparkled. Keeping Jinx a secret wasn't going to be easy.

Trix had spent most of last night in her room playing with Jinx. Mum and Dad thought she might be getting sick when she passed on dessert and a film on the telly. But it was easier being alone with Jinx – especially after he'd played hide and seek in Mum's shoes, climbed the lounge curtains, and pounced on the dining room table, sending the cutlery flying. And her dad sneezed like crazy when Jinx was close by. Jinx was a cheeky little kitten, but there was already a bond between them, just like Lulu had said there would be.

Trix kneeled down next to Jinx. "Please, please, please, be good, Jinx," she begged, petting his sparkling soft fur. Jinx blinked his yellow eyes at Trix as if he understood.

"Talking to yourself again, weirdo!" Oscar said, slamming the front door. Trix sprang to her feet.

"I have to talk to someone intelligent every once in a while," Trix said and stuck out her tongue. It wasn't really ten-year-old behaviour, but sometimes her brother's annoying antics made her do silly things.

"Yeah, since you usually talk to *stupid* Holly," Oscar said and kicked the flowers as he raced ahead. "I don't see why I have to walk to school with you two every day."

"You walk with us because Mum and Dad say you have to," Trix said and grabbed the collar of Oscar's Little Witching uniform. She pulled him back from the road. "Watch what you're doing!"

Jinx batted at the bobbing flowers and leaned in to sniff them. He was so cute. Trix's frustration with her little brother instantly faded. Having a kitten was exactly as wonderful as she'd thought it would be.

"Hi, Trix!" Holly called as she walked out of her front door. "Hi, Oscar," she said less enthusiastically. She looked both ways before crossing the street and raced over to Trix. "Watch this! I call it Holly's Magically Appearing Money. Nothing here!" Holly waved her hand in front of Trix. "But what's this?" Holly reached towards Trix's left ear.

Trix felt something hit her shoulder and then clatter to the kerb. "Drat and double drat!" Holly said. "I've been practising all night. I did it perfectly this morning."

"I believe you," Trix said, spotting the pound coin at the same time as Oscar.

"Look what I found!" Oscar said as he snatched up the coin.

"That's Holly's!" Trix ran after Oscar. Holly chased after Trix and Jinx scampered after them all as fast as his paws would take him.

Trix tackled Oscar to the ground. "Got it!" she said, wrestling the coin from Oscar's fist.

"Thanks, Trix!" Holly said, taking the coin and trying the trick again. She didn't drop it this time, but there was nothing magical about the coin's appearance. Trix could see the coin pinched between Holly's fingers the whole time.

"That's pretty good," Trix told Holly.

"That was rubbish!" Oscar blurted.

Holly's lip quivered.

"Don't listen to him," Trix said and set off towards school. "What does he know?"

When they reached the foot of Witching Hill, they double-crossed their fingers and then linked arms. Holly shut her eyes, and Trix led her forwards. Trix had told Holly that crossed fingers and arms would protect her from the scary old house that sat at the top of the hill, but Holly still didn't like to look. They used to have to cross to the opposite side of the road too, but Holly was slowly conquering her fear. Trix was sure that by the time they started Year Six, Holly would be ready to pass with her eyes open.

The house looked as if a toddler had constructed it from building blocks. There was a round tower on one side and two three-storey blocks that didn't line up properly. The windows were cracked and some were boarded up. Weeds covered the paving stones that led to the front door. Even when the sun was shining, the house still looked dark and shadowy.

Trix liked the old house. It was big with loads of places to explore. She liked to imagine that a captured princess lived in the

tower and a friendly ghost held tea parties for
the town goblins.

"Scaredy cats!" Oscar teased and ran ahead
up the hill. "You're afraid of a little old
haunted house!"

"We aren't scared, just careful," Holly
replied, opening one eye and then the other.

"And cats aren't scared, they are brave, isn't that right—" Trix was going to say 'Jinx' but stopped herself just in time. She'd almost blown her secret already.

"Right," Holly said.

Jinx raced over and pounced on Oscar's shoes as if to demonstrate his bravery. Oscar cried out at the fierce invisible kitten attack. He shook his leg and Jinx scampered away. Trix tried hard not to laugh.

"It's just a stupid old house," Oscar said, picking up a rock and tossing it towards the house.

"Cut that out, Oscar," Trix told her brother. "That was someone's home once."

"I know for a fact that house is haunted." Oscar planted his fists on his hips. "Scary witches live there. They have warts on their noses and long stringy hair."

"Don't be silly," Trix said and rubbed a finger over her nose to check for warts.

"You'll be sorry if you ever go near that house," Oscar said and headed in the direction of Little Witching Primary School.

"Do you really think horrible witches live there?" Holly asked.

"No, I don't," Trix said. *But there's a non-horrible one living across the street from you!* she added in her head.

Chapter Eight

So many shoes! Jinx thought as he, Trix and Holly approached the bus stop. He loved Trix's trainers. One was black and the other white. Just like my spots! Jinx thought. Holly had funny brown buckled shoes. Jinx rubbed against Holly's ankle and she jumped.

"What's the matter?" Jinx's witch asked her friend. Being with Trix made Jinx's tummy turn happy somersaults. He rolled around on the ground

at Trix's feet.

"I felt something brush my leg," Holly said, stopping to rub her ankle.

Jinx had liked Holly from the first moment he met her. Some people were cat people. They were bouncy and curious like Holly. And some people were more like lizards – like Trix's little brother. Jinx scampered over to three matching pairs of shiny pink shoes standing at the bus stop. He smelled roses and sneezed. These shoes belonged to the witches from the Enchanted Grove School for Girls. They were like pink lizards.

And there was Rascal. He'd just become a familiar to one of the pink lizards. He snuffled over to Jinx and gave him a nudge. Why did Rascal have so many wrinkles? Jinx swiped at the pug's nose. He didn't want to hurt him, just touch one of those wrinkles.

"Jinx, no!" Trix cried. Those words made Jinx's ears flatten. He didn't like that tone of voice. It felt like getting caught in the rain. Jinx hated being wet.

"What did you say?" Holly asked Trix.

"Jinx-O! I was thinking and, well, maybe that could be your new magical word. Try your trick again," Trix said quickly. Jinx thought she was talking gibberish.

"Um, I'm not sure," Holly whispered. "I don't want to do the trick now, not when those Enchanted Grove girls might see. Maybe after we've passed their bus stop."

"Oh, yeah, right." Trix nodded and glared at Jinx. His tail twitched. He knew what that look meant and he was trying to behave, he really was, but something came over him. He couldn't explain it. He needed to jump on Rascal's curly tail.

WOOF! WOOF! Rascal barked.

Jinx hissed and dived for the shelter of the shiny shoes.

"Wait, no!" Trix lunged for Jinx but missed and landed with a splash right in a muddy puddle!

That puddle hadn't been there a minute ago. It hadn't even been raining. Jinx looked from the shiny pink shoes up to the rosy-smelling lizard. He remembered that she had tried to choose him as her familiar before he could pick Trix. Jinx hissed at Stella. She had used magic to make that puddle for Trix. She was breaking the rules and using magic that Lulu hadn't taught them. And witches were only supposed to use magic to help people. Stella was not being helpful.

"Can't you control your cat?" Stella demanded, stepping over Trix.

"What are you talking about?" Trix asked, standing up and looking around.

Jinx nodded. Oh, Trix was so clever! Only witches could see him. What a funny trick Trix was playing on Stella!

"Your cat!" Stella shouted and pointed at Jinx. Every non-witch at the bus stop looked at Stella as if she were crazy. "Never mind," Stella huffed and flipped her hair over her shoulder. The Enchanted Grove bus pulled to the kerb, and Stella quickly jumped on board, followed by her two pink lizard friends.

Trix smiled at Jinx as she shook the water from her school uniform.

"What was she talking about?" Holly asked as the Enchanted Grove bus pulled away.

Trix pretended to tie her shoes but gave Jinx a stroke instead. "I have no idea," Trix said. Jinx could feel his spots sparkling.

Chapter Nine

*P**link! Plink!*
    Holly's fifty-pence coin bounced
from the lunch-room table to the floor. Jinx
batted at the spinning coin. Trix had to stifle
a laugh. Holly would think she was laughing
at her failed magic trick when in fact she was
laughing at Jinx's antics. The invisible kitten
was bounding from table to table, inspecting
every rucksack, lunch box, and shoe.

"You've almost got it," Trix told Holly. She picked up the coin and sneaked in a tickle of Jinx's chin. "One more time."

Holly took the coin and concealed it in her palm. The trick was simple. She had to slip the tip of the coin between two fingers so the coin was only visible to her. Then she needed to flick the coin up with her thumb with a flourish. The whole movement had to be done in a blink so she could appear to be pulling the coin out of an ear, nose, mouth, pocket or even thin air.

"Maybe try it in slow motion this time," Trix instructed. "If you get the movement right then you can speed it up."

"Watch and be amazed," Holly waved her hands. "Well, sort of amazed." Holly reached her hand behind Trix's ear and said, "Abracadabra." The coin seemed to appear from thin air.

Holly gasped in excitement. "I did it!" She flipped the coin in the air, caught it and tucked it back in her blazer pocket. People looked in her direction and Holly instantly slouched in her chair as if she were trying to make herself disappear.

"Holly the Magnificent!" Trix cheered. Jinx leaped onto the table to see what all the fuss was about.

"Trixibelle Morgan and Holly Duffy." It was Miss Abernathy. She had a way of making your name sound like a reprimand. "Hello, girls," Miss Abernathy said as she strolled over to their table. "Would you like to tell me what all the excitement is about?"

"Well, miss, Holly did a brilliant magic trick. She made a coin appear. She wants to be a magician." When she got nervous, Trix's talking-switch automatically flicked to 'on'. She pressed her lips shut tight.

"I'd love to see this wonderful trick, Holly," Miss Abernathy said, focusing her headmistress eyes on Holly like lasers. Holly turned thirteen-and-a-half shades of red.

"Go on, Holly," Trix encouraged. "Show her." Trix noticed a few of the students staring. Maybe this would prove to them once and for all that Holly was really special.

Holly fumbled with the coin. Her hands were shaking. The coin plinked to the floor, and Holly disappeared under the table searching for it.

Trix had to do something to save her best friend. "You know how magicians are," she said loudly to Miss Abernathy. "They mustn't give away their secrets."

"I can certainly appreciate artistic integrity," Miss Abernathy said.

Trix thought that was good, but she wasn't really sure.

"Holly's timing is impeccable," Miss Abernathy continued. Trix nodded as if she knew what Miss Abernathy's big word meant. "I was about to put a sign-up sheet on the noticeboard for the inaugural Little Witching and Enchanted Grove Schools Talent Show. It's a fundraising event for the local RSPCA." Miss Abernathy wrote Holly's name at the top of a sheet of paper. "Holly the Great can perform her magic trick at the talent show." Miss Abernathy smiled at Trix and added, "With her assistant, Trix, of course."

Miss Abernathy marched to the front of the cafeteria and made an announcement about the talent show. An excited buzz filled the air and several people rushed over to sign their names under Holly's.

"The coast is clear," Trix told Holly, who was still hiding under the table.

Holly slunk back into her chair. Her face had turned an all-new shade of neon red and she looked as if she might cry.

"I can't do magic on stage in front of an audience," Holly said. "This is the worst thing ever. Even worse than the time you convinced me to actually eat the mud pies we'd baked in Mum's new oven."

Trix scooted her chair closer to Holly's. "You *can* do this, Holly, and I can help. All we need is a super magical trick." Trix spotted her invisible kitten lapping up some spilled milk on a nearby table. "That's it!" Trix said. Holly looked at Trix as if she'd sprouted eagle wings and a clown nose. "Why don't you perform a disappearing act?"

"I have seen a cabinet in one of my magic books," Holly said. "The magician's assistant gets inside and then vanishes." Trix could tell Holly was starting to get a tiny bit excited about the idea. "Maybe my mum can build it for me," Holly went on, but then she fell silent, as if the sound had been sucked from her body. "Drat and double drat!" she said at last. "I will never be able to stand up in front of all those people. This is going to be a disaster."

Chapter Ten

Trix stood in front of the last bookcase at the very back of the library. For a second, she felt silly. She still couldn't believe she was a witch. Part of her thought she'd dreamed everything, but then Jinx appeared at her side and gave a loud *meow!* The bookcase flickered and transformed into a door. Jinx scampered in.

The magic classroom beyond glowed

orange. Smoke was bubbling from the cauldron.

"Hello, Trix and Jinx!" It was Lulu but she didn't look like a librarian. She was dressed in her glamorous witchy clothes. Her wavy, silvery-white hair shimmered and bounced around her shoulders as she stirred the cauldron. "I thought I'd whip up a batch of my Tasteriffic potion. I heard the lunch ladies were making their Tuna-Broccoli Surprise Casserole tomorrow."

Trix swallowed hard, remembering the nauseating combination. It had taken two chocolate bars and an entire pack of peppermint gum to erase that horrible flavour from her taste buds.

"One drop of my potion and the surprise is that it actually tastes good!" Lulu beamed.

Jinx raced over to Lulu. His black and white spots sparkled and swirled as he purred.

"Good to see you too, Jinx!" Lulu said. "Oh, really?" she seemed to be responding to Jinx. "That's wonderful. I'm so pleased." Lulu turned to Trix. "Jinx says you are purr-fect!"

Jinx dashed off to chase a spider that had escaped from a glass jar filled with silvery thread and marked *Sticky Spiderweb*.

"You're early." Lulu turned her attention to Trix. "Is there something on your mind?"

"I wonder if maybe, well, if . . ." The words tangled on Trix's tongue. She wanted to help her best friend with her magic trick, so she'd decided she was going to ask Lulu how to make things disappear. "I wondered if you could teach us—"

"Good afternoon, miss!" Stella and her friends swished into the room followed swiftly by pug, cat, owl and lavender rat. They looked like the weirdest parade Trix had ever seen. Now she couldn't ask Lulu her question, not in front of the other girls, especially Stella.

"Hello, my lovely little witches and frightfully friendly familiars," Lulu said, greeting each girl with an air-kiss and each familiar with a kindly scratch.

As Stella passed Trix, she whispered, "Already need some extra tutoring, Trix?"

Trix wanted to say something snarky back to Stella, but she knew it would probably only get her into trouble. She'd learned that from name-calling matches with Oscar. Mum usually sent them both to their rooms.

"Today, we will learn the art of . . ." Lulu spun, and the lacy edges of her long black gown twirled. She vanished in a puff of smoke. "Disappearing!" Lulu's voice said from an unknown location.

Trix sneezed. The smoke tickled her nose. *How did Lulu know that was what I was going to ask?*

"I am a fairy godmother, after all," Lulu's voice whispered in Trix's ear. Trix jumped in surprise as Lulu materialised right behind her. "The trick to any magical spell is finding the words that work for you." Lulu flicked her wrist and clicked her fingers and – *poof!* – a sturdy wooden table appeared in front of them. All the familiars hopped, ran or flew over and took their places in front of their witches. "Your magic is not very powerful yet, so you will only be able to make simple things disappear."

"You mean simple things like Trix," Stella muttered.

"No, not like people," Lulu said, and glared at Stella, who was trying to look innocent. "Making *people* disappear is much more complex. It's better to try your spell on things like these." She tossed a handful of gold coins into the air and one magically settled in front of each witch. "I can't tell you the rhyme that will work for you. You must discover it for yourself. That's part of the magic!"

In less than a minute, Stella had uttered a spell that rhymed *vanish* with *banish*. To show off, she made the coin disappear and reappear again and again.

"Very good, Stella," Lulu said, snatching back the gold coin.

"Thank you, miss," Stella said and curtsied. "Easy peasy!"

"Maybe you should try something bigger." With a flick of Lulu's wrist and a click of her fingers, a huge book plunked down in front of Stella. Trix could see it was the 'S' volume of an old encyclopaedia. *S for Stella*, Trix thought, but then the book flipped open. *Show Off* was printed across the top of the page with a photo of Stella underneath.

All the girls tried not to laugh. Stella's toothy smile dipped into a scowl.

"Humble witches make the best fairy godmothers," Lulu said and Trix secretly smiled. "Keep trying, everyone! Practice makes practically perfect!"

Trix glared at her coin, which so far had refused to disappear. She'd tried rhyming *coin* and *join*. Then she'd tried *gone* and *swan*, which had momentarily morphed the Queen's image into a swan and back again. Trix noticed that Pippa, Becka and Cara's coins, and even Stella's encyclopaedia, had all disappeared. Everyone was staring at her.

Trix took a deep breath and squinted at the golden coin. *"Little coin, I am sincere,"* Trix said. Stella coughed and Trix momentarily lost her concentration. *"I-I want to see you disappear,"* she finished. The coin flickered and faded, but she could still see its outline.

"Lovely rhyme, Trix," Lulu said "I think all you need is focus. Let's try it together."

They repeated Trix's rhyme and – *poof!* – the gold coin disappeared.

"Practise your disappearing spells tonight, but remember – no one must see you performing magic," Lulu said and, with a sweep of her arms and a jangle of her bracelets, she was gone. "Tootles until tomorrow!"

Trix sighed. How was she ever going to help Holly if she couldn't even perform a simple spell by herself?

Stella knocked Trix's shoulder as she passed. "You'll never be a fairy godmother. You're barely a witch," Stella said and made herself disappear. Trix couldn't help hoping she wouldn't come back – ever!

Chapter Eleven

"Hi, Mr and Mrs Duffy," Trix called as she let herself into Holly's house after dinner that night. She'd left Jinx curled up asleep on her bed. She hoped he would stay out of trouble.

"Hi, Trix!" Mrs Duffy said, waving her paintbrush. She was splattered with bright blue paint and stood next to a blue cabinet that was the size and shape of a phone box.

"Maybe you can cheer Holly up. Miss Abernathy called and told us all about the talent show. We're so excited, but Holly's acting like it's the end of the world."

Holly was curled up on the sofa next to her dad, who was sewing something.

"I knew this old costume would come in handy," he said, holding up a silky blue cape. *Holly the GR* was spelled out in yellow sequins.

"That looks amazing, Mr D," Trix said. Holly groaned and curled tighter into a ball.

"Look at this!" Mrs Duffy said, sliding back the curtain of the big blue cabinet. "I call it the Super-duper Disappearing Box." She stepped inside. "Watch and be amazed!" Mrs Duffy said in her best magician's voice. She pressed something on the inside of the box. "Voila!" A panel at the back of the box slid away. "Now you see me . . ." Mrs Duffy stepped behind the panel and pressed the button again. The panel slid shut. "Now you don't," came her muffled voice.

Trix clapped. "That's fantastic!" She waited for Mrs Duffy to reappear.

The cabinet rocked back and forth. "Um, Trix, can you give that panel a little shove?" Mrs Duffy shouted from the secret hiding space. "I seem to be stuck."

Trix found the button and pressed it again. Nothing happened, so she pried open the panel with her fingernails.

"OK, it needs a little work, but it's going to be super once it's finished," Mrs Duffy said as she climbed out of the cabinet. "Why don't you girls go up to Holly's room and practise the act?"

"What am I going to do?" Holly flopped on her bed. "My grandparents have already booked train tickets and Dad's ordered a video camera off the internet especially to film his 'little magician's debut'. There is no way I'll ever get out of this now."

"Come on, Holly," Trix said. "It'll be fun."

Holly tied the sleeves of her frilly pink nightgown around her neck to make a cape. "Introducing Holly the Grim. For my first trick, I will embarrass myself in front of everyone at Little Witching." She grabbed her hairbrush and swirled it over her head like a magic wand. "And for my next trick, I will make myself disappear for ever." Holly dived under the pile of covers and clothes that were mounded on her bed. "Ta da!" she shouted.

Trix laughed. Holly poked her head out of the mess. "I can't do this!"

"Yes, you can," Trix said, tossing aside T-shirts and blue jeans to uncover her best friend. Trix wished she knew a magic spell to give Holly more confidence. Holly's guinea pig, Fuzzy-Wuzzle-Be, squeaked in his cage. "See, even Fuzzy wants you to perform," Trix said, poking a finger though Fuzzy's cage and giving him a stroke. Fuzzy squeaked again and dashed into his den, which Holly had created out of a tissue box. That's when Trix spotted her sparkling kitten hiding among the pile of clothes on Holly's bed. She still wasn't used to her magical familiar showing up whenever and wherever he felt like it.

"I may have to fake cowpox on Friday." Holly sat up. "I'm feeling a bit moo-serable."

Trix laughed. "I think you mean *chicken*pox."

"I need a bigger farm animal to get out of the talent show," Holly said as she dotted her face with the orange crush lip gloss from her nightstand. "You think my parents will buy it?" She collapsed back on her bed dramatically.

"Not a chance," Trix said and wiped the orange goo off Holly's face with a tissue. "Let's at least give the trick a try. We can use your wardrobe in place of the Super-duper Disappearing Box." Trix climbed into Holly's wardrobe, pushed all her clothes aside and shut the door. "Say some magic words or something and let's see what happens."

"My name is Holly the Not-So-Great and I will make my best friend, and this whole stupid idea of being a magician, disappear!" Holly announced and tapped the side of the wardrobe with her hairbrush.

Trix was suddenly struck by a brilliant idea. If she could make herself disappear for a second, maybe Holly would see that the trick could work and have the confidence to do the talent show.

As Holly mumbled a string of magic and not-so-magic words, Trix whispered, "*A little help for Holly here. Make her friend disappear*." It was a terrible rhyme, but she hoped it would work anyway.

Holly opened the wardrobe door. "This trick is rubbish," she told Trix. Holly was looking right at her, so clearly Trix's stupid spell hadn't worked. "Maybe you could help me pack and Fuzzy and I can run away," Holly went on. She kneeled down. "We could hide out at your house." Holly opened Fuzzy's cage and reached inside. "Where's Fuzzy?" she said, feeling around the cage. "He's gone!"

Trix's disappointment that her spell hadn't worked instantly turned to horror that it had! Had she made Fuzzy disappear? Fuzzy was Holly's friend too. Trix realised she should have specified best *human* friend in her spell. In fact, she shouldn't have used her magic. She didn't really understand how it worked.

"Fuzzy-Wuzzle-Be!" Holly called, searching her room.

Trix's feeling of dread multiplied like bubbles in a bubble bath when she heard a guinea pig squeal and saw Jinx racing out of the bedroom door.

"I think he went this way," Trix said and raced after Jinx. How was she ever going to find an invisible guinea pig being chased by an invisible kitten?

Chapter Twelve

Jinx followed as Fuzzy trotted down the hall. Jinx was surprised at how fast the guinea pig could move. Clearly Fuzzy liked a game of chase as much as Jinx did.

Jinx meowed triumphantly when he caught up with Fuzzy at the top of the stairs. Now Fuzzy would be 'it'. That's how the game worked. He gave Fuzzy a playful nudge. Fuzzy squealed as he tumbled down the stairs.

Brown. White. Black. Brown. White. Black.
Jinx watched the colourful guinea pig spin all the
way to the bottom. Jinx bounced down the stairs
after Fuzzy with a meow of delight.

"Jinx! Jinx!" Trix was whispering in a way that
felt more like a shout.

Jinx glanced up the stairs. What fun, Jinx
thought, Trix is playing too!

Fuzzy shook his furry head and scampered off.
The chase was on again.

Jinx leaped on the sofa and quickly inspected
what Holly's dad was making. Jinx was
momentarily mesmerised by the yellow sequins.
He hoped he might have a sparkly collar one day.

He loved sparkly things! He batted at the cape's blue ribbon that was bouncing as Holly's dad stitched the last few sequins on the 'T'. And then he spotted a whole bowl of yellow sequins. They seemed to twinkle like stars. He took a flying leap and . . .

Splat!

Jinx was covered in sequins. He rolled one way and then the other. The sequins swished in the bowl and tickled as they stuck to his fur. Fuzzy sniffed at Jinx and then dashed towards the big blue box.

"Oh, no!" Trix yelled when she spotted Jinx. She dived towards him but he slipped out of her grasp, leaving most of the sequins in her hands.

"Sorry, Mr D," Trix said, standing up and dusting sequins off her blue jeans. "I'll clean this up. I thought I saw Fuzzy-Wuzzle-Be."

"Is that hamster missing again?" Holly's dad asked.

"It's a guinea pig, darling, not a hamster," Holly's mum corrected, accidentally flicking blue paint everywhere.

Hurrah! Jinx thought. Makeover time! He

admired Fuzzy's black and white fur, now dotted with yellow sequins and blue paint spots.

"Jinx, please stop," Trix whispered as Jinx followed Fuzzy though a puddle of paint and then zigzagged around the room.

"What . . ." was all Holly's dad could say when he looked up and saw the state of the lounge. Blue paint and yellow sequins were everywhere.

"How . . ." Holly's mum added.

Jinx giggled and Fuzzy squealed when they saw the funny trail of paw prints behind them. They'd done a really awesome job. Jinx tilted his head. If you looked at it this way, it looked like a bouquet of flowers. But if you looked at it that way – Jinx rolled on his back and stared upside down at the pattern of blue paw prints – it looked like a sea of wonky stars.

"Where is Fuzzy?" It was Trix.

Jinx jumped to his feet and knocked heads with Trix, who was on all fours. Had Trix lost her mind? Fuzzy was sitting right there in front of her. Jinx kept forgetting he was invisible and Fuzzy was too. So funny, new witches didn't always understand their magic. He raised his paw and pointed. Fuzzy was reappearing. Brown. White. Black. Brown. White. Black.

"I found Fuzzy-Wuzzle-Be!" Trix picked up the squealing guinea pig.

"How did you get all the way down here?" Holly asked as she leaped from the stairs and skidded to a stop, completely smudging Jinx and Fuzzy's painting. "What a mess you've made, Fuzzy." Holly took Fuzzy from Trix and snuggled him.

"There are two sets of paw prints," Holly's mum said, dropping her paintbrush in a spray of blue.

Trix grabbed a nearby rag and began to wipe the wooden floor. "Nope, only Fuzzy's paws. They're smudged because he was running."

Trix is so smart! Jinx thought and leaped onto the rag so Trix was spinning him around as she was cleaning the last of the paint from the floor.

"I'd better get home," Trix said, wiggling a finger at Jinx to follow.

"What about my trick?" Holly asked.

"We'll practise more tomorrow," Trix said, giving Holly a hug and Fuzzy a stroke. "But you're going to be great!"

Holly's dad held up the cape, now swimming in sequins. "That's what the cape says, after all."

Jinx scampered out of the door behind Trix.

"All the practice in the world and I'm never going to be a great witch," Trix told Jinx sadly.

Jinx wished and wished and wished that Trix could understand him. He raced around in circles and meowed at the top of his lungs.

"You're funny," Trix said, giving Jinx a kiss on his head.

You are a great witch! Jinx thought. Or you will be some day.

Chapter Thirteen

The long black tail of Trix's cat clock swished from side to side. *Tick! Tock!* Trix felt as if the time was passing in exclamation marks. Her mind was too busy thinking to sleep. She counted the cat clock's meows. Twelve! It was midnight – the witching hour!

Trix threw back her covers. She looked up

at the not-quite-so-full moon. Two nights ago she had seen Lulu and Sparkles flying across the night sky. She was supposed to be a witch, but her only magical power was making a super-duper magical mess. Look at the chaos she'd created by making Fuzzy-Wuzzle-Be accidentally disappear.

Trix could see that Holly's bedroom light was still on. Her friend was wearing her magician's cape and flicking her hairbrush like a wand at the wardrobe. She must be practising her magic trick. *Some fairy godmother I'll be*, Trix thought. *I can't even help my best friend.*

Eventually Lulu would realise she'd made a mistake. Maybe Trix should quit fairy-godmother training before she got thrown out.

Suddenly Jinx jumped onto the windowsill and then disappeared before Trix's very eyes! *Now that's magic!* Trix thought. *What's that crazy kitten up to?*

Jinx reappeared in Trix's front garden. He rolled and tumbled in Mum's roses, his fur glowing in the moonlight. He looked up at Trix and meowed before dashing down the street.

Trix didn't think. She had to go after Jinx. She quickly dressed and tied her long, curly hair in two bunches. She caught sight of herself in the mirror. She didn't look like Lulu or any of the Enchanted Grove girls. Her bunches were lopsided. Her shoes didn't match. Her favourite white sweatshirt had two huge green smudges where Oscar had left his green socks in the white washing pile. Even her blue jeans had several holes where she and Holly had played fashion designer and cut out circles, creating the first ever polka-dot jeans. Mum had not been impressed.

Once outside, Trix easily found Jinx. His glowing spots were clearly visible, bouncing up Witching Hill. He was heading straight for the haunted house. Trix slowed. She liked the old house, but at night she had to admit it looked spooky. She told herself to stop being silly. It was just a sad old house, but her tummy wouldn't listen.

"Jinx!" Trix called. "Jinx, come back here."
When Jinx reached the front door of
the haunted house, he raised his paw as if
waving and then disappeared in a burst of
sparkles.

If she lost her familiar, Trix was pretty
sure that would be the end of her dream
of becoming a fairy godmother – once and
for all. So Trix summoned all her courage
and mentally morphed the butterflies in her
stomach into one brave, strong lion. She
marched right up to the house. There was no
sign of Jinx anywhere.

The lion in her stomach was feeling more

like a kitty cat. She had to hurry before the butterflies came back. She used the sleeve of her sweatshirt to wipe an eyeball-sized circle in one of the dirty front windows, and the whole window seemed to magically clear so that she could see into the house.

Trix gasped. "Creeping cats!"

She couldn't be seeing what she was seeing. Maybe she was dreaming. She pinched herself to check. *Ouch!* She definitely wasn't dreaming.

She rubbed her eyes and looked again.

Trix squealed with excitement.

On the outside, the house looked like it might topple over. But on the *inside*, the house was shiny and new, all glass and chrome with a big crystal chandelier lighting up a gleaming ballroom. The room was packed with women who looked as though they had stepped out of a glossy fashion magazine. They all wore glamorous gowns and Trix could hear the hum of conversation. The women were speaking in a number of different languages. Trix guessed they had

come from all around the world. They were
laughing and dancing and drinking bubbly
drinks. They looked absolutely magical!

Trix spotted a flash of silvery hair weaving through the crowd. It was Lulu! She was wearing a long, silky emerald-green gown with a necklace and earrings to match. Magic was sparkling all around. Trix realised that all those women must be fairy godmothers!

Trix ducked out of sight. She looked down at her dirty sweatshirt and tattered jeans. If this was how the world's fairy godmothers looked, then Trix knew for a fact that she could never, ever – not in a million years – be one of them. The last sparkles of her courage melted away. Trix felt that gooey feeling that always came before tears.

Chapter Fourteen

Oh, it hurt Jinx to see Trix so sad. His tail drooped. His whiskers frowned. He felt his spots lose their shine. He had hoped that seeing Magic Mansion would cheer up Trix, but instead it had made her even sadder.

Jinx materialised at Trix's feet and rubbed up against her legs. Trix jumped.

"Oh, it's you," Trix said and wiped her eyes. "I was worried about you, Jinx."

Jinx felt magic in the air. He turned just as Lulu magically appeared by Trix's side.

"Jinx Jingle Jangle, you naughty kitty!" she said, but her eyes twinkled. "You know witches-in-training aren't supposed to come to Magic Mansion until the Sisterhood of Magic Ball."

The kitten bowed his head and tucked his tail between his legs. He was very sorry for breaking the rules, but Trix had lost her shine. Lulu had to see that. Wasn't it a familiar's job to keep his or her witch feeling magical?

"Yes, yes, you're right, Jinx." Lulu turned to Trix. "I see what you mean. Something will have to be done."

Jinx sat right on Trix's black trainer. He thumped his tail once, twice. He felt a tear plop onto his fur.

"Lulu, I'm sorry," Trix said and sniffed.

"You have nothing to be sorry for." Lulu lifted Trix's chin. "Jinx wanted to cheer you up, but I'm not sure why someone as lovely and magical as you should be feeling so sad."

"Thank you for all your training," Trix said and glanced in the window. "But I can't be a witch. And

if only the best witches become fairy godmothers,
I will never, ever be a fairy godmother. I don't
belong here."

How can Trix say that? Jinx stepped back a few
feet and then launched himself into Trix's arms. He
sparkled and purred. Trix was a witch. She was his
witch.

"I love Jinx," Trix said and snuggled Jinx closer
and kissed the top of his head. "But look at me. I
will never be one of those glamorous women." She
nodded towards Magic Mansion.

"Oh, is that all that's bothering you?" Lulu said. She put an arm around Trix's shoulders. Lulu's touch made Jinx feel swirly-twirly, like sliding down a rainbow. "The best thing about being a witch is that you see the best in people. This is how you see us," Lulu turned Trix and Jinx towards the window so they could see all the beautiful fairy godmothers, "but we're not that different from you." Lulu cast a spell. The glass clouded for a second and then became shiny clean. The image through the window changed. "All fairy godmothers look marvellous when they are at Magic Mansion, but this is how they look in the real world."

The women in the ballroom were still sparkling and magical, but they were every shape and size. They didn't look perfect and Jinx liked them better. Lulu had transformed back into a librarian with her hair in a messy bun and her clothes a mismatch of patterns and colours.

"You have the gift of magic," Lulu told Trix. "With a little time and training, you will be a wonderful witch and, I'm sure, you will become one of the best fairy godmothers the Sisterhood of Magic has ever known." Lulu placed kisses on both of Trix's cheeks and one on Jinx's head. "Rock-a-bye. Rock-a-bye. Slumber and snore. Snuggle in bed and worry no more."

A breeze rippled through Jinx's fur. The next thing he knew, he was tucked up in bed with Trix. And the best part was that Trix's face was shiny with a smile.

"I promise you, Jinx Jingle Jangle," Trix whispered into Jinx's pointy ear, "that I will not let you and Lulu down. I will be the best witch ever –

and maybe even a fairy godmother one day." Trix glanced out of her bedroom window as the light in Holly's bedroom went out. "And for my first trick, I will help my best friend Holly wow everyone at the talent show!"

Chapter Fifteen

Trix and Holly peeked through the fuzzy red curtains pulled tight across the Little Witching Primary School stage.

"It's only the school hall," Trix told Holly as they looked out at the rows and rows of benches slowly filling with people. Holly's parents and grandparents lined the front row. Miss Abernathy had strung hundreds of silver stars and twinkle lights from the ceiling. It did make the school hall look a little magical.

Holly smiled. "You're right. I can do this," she said, but Trix noticed a slight tremor in her voice.

"We've practised all week," Trix turned up her enthusiasm to a hundred watts. "You did it perfectly twice yesterday. You look like a real magician and I look like a comic book character."

Holly giggle-snorted. Trix's parents weren't nearly as handy as Holly's. Holly had a top hat and matching cape over her best blue jeans, and a bright yellow T-shirt to match the sequins on her cape. Her mum had even surprised her with beautiful new, bright yellow, fancy shoes. Trix, on the other hand, was wearing her old, red one-piece swimming costume with a black mini-skirt. She had jazzed her outfit up with the tights her Aunt Belle had sent her from a designer shop in London. They had red roses painted all over them. Mum had turned an apron into a short sort-of cape, which wasn't exactly the same red as her swimming costume, and she'd pinned Trix's hair up in a sophisticated bun with loads of curls framing her face. Mum had even let Trix borrow a pair of her grandma's old clip-on hoop earrings.

"Let's finish getting ready," Trix said to Holly and led the way out of the school hall.

Miss Abernathy had turned Miss Eaton and Mr Powell's classrooms into dressing rooms. She'd placed gold stars on the doors with *Little Witching Primary School* spelled out in glitter on one and *Enchanted Grove School for Girls* on the other.

Up ahead Trix saw the worst sight imaginable. A grizzly bear or land-roving killer shark would have been more welcome. Trix picked up her pace, dragging Holly behind her.

"What's the mat—" Holly started but it was too late. They were face to face with Stella, Pippa and Cara – or The Pink Panthers as their fuchsia T-shirts proclaimed.

"Aw, look what we have here," Stella sing-songed. "A wannabe magician and her sad-o assistant." She tilted her head in that cking way of all evil villains.

The Enchanted Grove girls laughed. Holly turned her own personal shade of fuchsia.

Trix was hot with anger. Her brain was bubbling with mean things to say. She wanted to hurt them as much as she could see they'd hurt her best friend. *Why do they have to be so mean?*

"Holly is a great magician," Trix said and took a protective step in front of Holly, shielding her from the mean-girl vibes. "You'll see. She has more talent in her top hat than you have in your whole stupid bodies."

Trix had to admit they looked amazing. They wore matching shirts, pink jeans and pink shoes.

"Come on, Holly!" Trix looped her arm through Holly's and walked away.

"Good luck, Holly the Great," Stella called.

Trix was more determined than ever to make sure Holly's performance was awesome. They had to show those girls. "Let's practise one more time," Trix told Holly.

"We can't. Dad already put the Super-duper Disappearing Box on the stage," Holly said, plopping onto the floor in the corner of the dressing room where all the other acts were busy getting ready. Parents were buzzing about, putting the final touches to costumes and props. Trix sank down next to Holly. She spotted Jinx scampering between a juggler and a saxophonist. He paused to bat at the coloured scarves the juggler was tossing into the air. Trix smiled at Jinx and wished for the millionth time that Holly could see her magical familiar. Jinx would certainly cheer up Holly.

Miss Abernathy appeared at the door to the Little Witching dressing room and clapped her hands twice to get everyone's attention. "We are about to begin." She beamed the too-big smile she always used when parents were around. "Parents, please take your seats. And students, prepare." She paused to make sure they were all listening. "I expect magic tonight!"

All the acts lined up in order of appearance

right outside the stage door. Unfortunately Holly was the very last act. The longer Holly waited, the more frightened she got. The Pink Panthers didn't seem nervous at all. They chatted and laughed like they always did.

As The Pink Panthers took the stage, Trix thought she heard Stella mumble a rhyming spell. Trix couldn't help but wonder how

much magic Stella had used to help her act. Trix and Holly tried not to listen, but they had to admit The Pink Panthers sang almost as well as the girl bands on the radio. Holly even tapped her toe in time to the music. The crowd clapped for one whole minute after they'd finished.

"Holly and Trix, you're next," Miss Abernathy waved them forwards.

"What if I make a fool of myself and everyone laughs?" Holly backed away from the stage door. "I'll have to move house and then we couldn't be best friends."

"Making everyone laugh is a great thing! You just have to make everyone laugh *with* you," Trix said, stepping up behind Holly. "And I will always be your best friend!" Trix nudged Holly forwards. Holly walked up the stairs and onto the stage without another word.

"Presenting . . ." Miss Abernathy called from the front of the stage. "Holly the Great and the Super-duper Disappearing Box!"

Trix took Holly's hand and led her to centre stage beside the Super-duper Disappearing Box. The spotlight flashed on, its white-hot light focused on Holly and Trix. Trix gulped as a sea of faces came into focus. Her body felt as if it had been invaded by a swarm of fireflies. There was the warm glow of excitement, but also the flutter of fear.

Chapter Sixteen

Trying not to move her lips so the audience couldn't see she was speaking, Trix whispered to Holly, "Pretend we're in your bedroom."

Holly nodded but stared wide-eyed at the audience. "When did all these people move into my house?"

Trix laughed. *That's it,* Trix thought. *Get Holly laughing and she'll forget to be scared.*

Trix stepped to the front of the stage. "For the first—"

"And only," Holly mumbled. Laughter bubbled up from the audience.

"And only time, Holly the Great will perform . . ." Trix nodded at Holly.

". . . the one and only trick I know," Holly said, her voice getting stronger. "If I'm honest, I'd like to make *myself* disappear."

More laughter. It seemed to cast a magical spell over Holly. She stood up straighter and even smiled a little.

"But instead I'm going to make all of *you* disappear," Holly said.

Trix's eyes widened. This wasn't the way they'd practised. *What was Holly doing?*

"Abracadabra," Holly said, loud and clear. She closed her eyes and turned her back to the audience. "See! You've all vanished."

Laughter rang out through the school hall. Holly had turned into a comedian.

"And now for the Super-duper Disappearing Box," Holly said and turned back to face the audience.

Trix stepped up next to the box. The trick's name was painted down the side. Trix swept her arm down the length of the box like she'd seen models do on the shopping channel.

"It's your average, ordinary, big blue box," Holly said and gave an exaggerated wink to the audience. "Nothing special or magical about it." Holly knocked on each side of the box to prove it was solid wood. "Unless you count the big yellow lettering that sort of gives the trick away."

"You are doing great," Trix told Holly as she took her place in the cabinet.

"I will make my assistant and best friend,

Trix, disappear," Holly announced. She drew the curtain across, hiding Trix from view. "She's a magician too. Just show her some chocolate and watch her make it disappear!"

Trix could hear Mum, Dad and Oscar laughing the loudest at that.

"I can still hear you, you know!" Trix shouted through the box to Holly.

"Can you disappear already?" Holly replied. They were both starting to have fun.

"You have to say the magic words," Trix shouted back.

Trix pushed the button like she had done in practice, but the secret panel was stuck. Sweat trickled down Trix's back. She tried to press the button again, but her hands were shaking.

Creeping cats!

"I'm going to use the most magical words of all," Holly declared, and then paused dramatically. "School's out for summer!" she shouted and everyone laughed. Everyone except Trix. She had been worried about Holly, but now *she* was the one who was going to ruin everything.

Holly threw back the curtain, expecting to reveal an empty box.

The audience gasped – not because of what they *didn't* see but because of what they *did*.

Trix.

Trix felt her face flush. She shrank away from the light, sure that she could hear Stella's loud laughter coming from the wings of the stage.

"Try it again," Trix whispered to Holly. The look in Holly's eyes told Trix that panic was setting in. "I promise it will work this time," Trix added.

As soon as the curtain closed, Trix tried the button again and again, but it was broken. She knew what she had to do. Trix concentrated as hard as she could. *If Lulu and Jinx believe in me, then I need to believe in myself*, Trix thought.

She closed her eyes and whispered a rhyme that seemed to magically appear in her brain: *"Holly, my best friend, have no fear. For I'm a witch and I* will *disappear."*

"Maybe it was my choice of magic words,"

Trix heard Holly saying to the crowd. Her voice was soft and shaky. "What's more magical than summertime?"

"Friendship," Trix said.

"True, blue friendship!" Holly called. "Now disappear, my friend, pretty please!"

Trix heard the curtain being drawn back and then loud applause. She opened one eye and then the other. She looked down at herself but, instead of her silly costume, Trix saw nothing. She'd done it. She'd made herself invisible using real magic!

Trix clapped the loudest as Holly bowed.

Trix's body tingled. Her trainers were starting to reappear.

"Close the curtain, Holly," Trix whispered.

Holly took one more bow and then closed the curtain.

"Abracadabra!" Holly shouted.

Trix crossed her fingers and toes. It wasn't very witchy but it was all she had time to do before Holly opened the curtain again.

Trix waved her hands in front of her face. She could see them now.

"We did it!" Holly swept Trix into a huge hug. The audience was on its feet, clapping and cheering. Holly took Trix's hand and they both bowed together.

Trix spotted Lulu the librarian standing at the back of the school hall. *Does she suspect that I used magic?* If she did, Trix knew she was going to be in big witchy trouble. But looking at Holly, Trix didn't care. Sure, she wanted to be a fairy godmother, but it was way more important that the world had finally seen how special her best friend really was. *That* was its own kind of magic.

Chapter Seventeen

Trix had to admit that she was a little nervous as she opened the secret door in the library on Monday afternoon. She gave Jinx a little stroke for good luck. Stella, Pippa, Cara, Becka and their familiars were already waiting in the magic classroom. Jinx raced over to greet Twitch, Sherlock, Tabby and even Rascal.

"Your band was really great at the talent show," Trix said to Stella, Pippa and Cara, who were wearing their Pink Panthers T-shirts.

"Thanks," Pippa said stepping away from Stella who was whispering something to Cara and Becka. "Your friend is really funny. I liked your act, too."

"Thanks," Trix said, looking around for Lulu.

"Greetings, my lovely little witches," Lulu said as she magically appeared in the centre of the room. "Magic up! I have something very important I must tell you."

The girls formed a circle with Lulu in the centre.

"Each time a witch-in-training masters one witchy lesson, she will get a lovely surprise," Lulu said, pointing to each girl. A smaller version of Lulu's pointy witch's hat appeared on each girl's head. The hats were black but decorated with ribbons and bows. A silvery sash draped itself across Trix's body. It was like the ones girls wore in beauty pageants. Trix could see that her classmates all wore sashes too.

"I will place a sparkling gem on your sash each time you succeed," Lulu continued. "Witches-in-training can also lose gems for misusing magic – casting a selfish spell, for example."

Trix couldn't look at Lulu. She hadn't been selfish with her magic, but she *had* performed a spell in the real world. She didn't want to disappoint Lulu, not after everything she'd said at Magic Mansion, and especially after Trix had decided, once and for all, that she wanted to be a fairy godmother one day. She liked how helping Holly had made her feel all happy inside.

"One witch has earned her first Sisterhood reward," Lulu said with a smile. Stella stepped forwards as if she knew she was the one. Even Trix had to admit that Stella was the best witch so far.

"Trixibelle Elizabeth Morgan, congratulations!" Lulu touched a point on Trix's sash near her shoulder. A beautiful shimmering pink gem appeared on her sash. When Trix stared at the shiny surface, she could swear she saw Holly's face reflected there.

"Trix helped her best friend Holly find confidence, like a real fairy godmother," Lulu said and gave Trix a hug. Jinx bounded over and wound himself around Trix's leg.

Pippa, Cara, Becka and even Stella circled Trix to see the sparkling jewel. "Well done!" they all said.

And Trix finally knew. This was what magic felt like!

Don't miss the next exciting adventure
in the *Magic Trix* series

Flying High

Available now!
Read on for a special preview of the first
chapter.

Chapter One

Trix leaned forwards and aimed her broom for the stars. She shot off like a rocket, bursting through a thick, fluffy mattress of clouds. Speeding through the clouds felt like being tickled by a thousand feathers. The wind whipped through her curly brown hair as she flew higher and higher and faster and faster until Little Witching was a twinkly blur below her.

Flying was the best feeling in the world.

At least she hoped it would be . . .

. . . when she learned how to do it.

Trix opened her eyes.

It was only a daydream. Her trainers – one black and one white – were firmly planted on the floor of the magic classroom hidden in the Little Witching Primary School library. Her dream of flying seemed as far away as Little Witching was from the dazzling rings of Saturn.

"My little witches, before we can fly we must create our vehicles!" Lulu exclaimed.

She waved her broom in the air and set her bracelets jingle-jangling. Lulu was their magical teacher from the Sisterhood of Magic. It was her job to teach Trix and the four other new witches – Stella, Pippa, Cara and Becka – the art of magic. The girls looked like proper witches with the tiny pointed hats Lulu had given them – but they had a lot to learn. The best and brightest witches would become fairy godmothers one day.

Was it only last week that Trix had turned ten and discovered she had the gift of magic? Trix still couldn't believe she was a witch with her own magical familiar – a black and white kitten named Jinx who was only visible to witches. She had to keep her new magical powers and her amazing invisible kitten a secret from everyone – even her best friend Holly.

"Witches fly on besoms," Lulu explained. She held the broom straight out in front of her. "A besom is a very special kind of broom. Like your magical rhyming spells, your besom will be unique to you. Once each

of you has created your very
own besom, we can start
flying lessons."

Trix's tummy got all fluttery
with the thought of actually flying.
She studied Lulu's besom. It had
silver and gold bands spaced up and
down the broom handle, matching
Lulu's bracelet-filled wrists.

"Um, what's it called again?" Pippa
asked. Her high blonde ponytail
flipped from side to side as she looked
from Lulu to the sticks in the centre of the
room that they would use to construct their
brooms.

Stella laughed, but it wasn't the nice kind
of laugh that friends share. Stella's laugh was
forced and seemed to be thrown like a ball of
stinky cheese. "It's called a besom, silly."

Pippa blushed. Her familiar, a lavender
rat named Twitch, climbed out of the pink
handbag that was slung over Pippa's shoulder.
Twitch scampered up Pippa's arm and curled
around her neck. "Thanks, Twitch," Pippa

whispered and brushed her cheek on the rat's soft lavender fur.

Trix knew how Pippa felt because Stella usually saved all her meanness for Trix. Stella, Cara and Pippa attended the Enchanted Grove School for Girls, and they *usually* stuck together.

"We do not call other people names, Stella," Lulu said and made Stella's name sound like a bad word. "Neither Pippa nor her question is silly. Questions are rainbows to knowledge." Lulu clapped her hands and returned to her witchy lesson. "There is no right or wrong way to create your besom. The only thing it has to do is fly. Now, let's get to work!"

Trix let her hand hover over the pile of long, thick branches that Lulu had supplied for the handle part of the broom. Her fingers tingled as she came to a crooked branch with bumps all over it. "This is it," she whispered to Jinx. She picked it up and noticed that the lines in the bark seemed to swirl.

Jinx helped Trix line up a bundle of sticks at one end of the handle. Trix carefully wove the twine in and out of the branches. Jinx batted at the ball of twine, chasing after it when it rolled away. As Trix worked, she noticed the twine change from a dull brown to a shimmering rainbow of colours. She must be doing something right!

"Finished!" Stella said and raised her perfect broom over her head. Trix noticed that she'd turned it nail-polish pink. "That was easy peasy! I'm ready to fly."

"We will fly when *everyone* has finished their besoms," Lulu said. "This is not a test of speed but of creativity." As Lulu inspected the other witches' brooms, Trix took a sneaky peek too. Cara and Becka were nearly finished. Their besoms looked like proper brooms – except the twine on Becka's broom was plaited like her own brown hair, and the end of Cara's broom was twice as bushy as everyone else's.

"Look at Pippa's!" Stella pointed and laughed. It seemed to Trix that Becka and Cara echoed Stella's laugh even before they'd looked in Pippa's direction.

Pippa had tied bunches of sticks up and down her broom. They looked like wooden bows spaced equally apart.

"I was just . . . It was only . . ." Pippa's face flushed again. "I was just experimenting. It was only a joke." She laughed, but Trix could tell it was a fake laugh – like the way Trix's parents laughed at one of her little brother Oscar's not-funny jokes.

"I think it looks really interesting," Trix told Pippa.

"Thanks, Trix," Pippa whispered, but she ripped the bunches of twigs from her broom and tied them at the end like everyone else had done.

"Gather round, my little witches and friendly familiars," Lulu said and waved the five girls and their familiars over. Her bracelets jangled and her silvery-white hair bounced at her shoulders. "Grab your besom

and hold it out in front of
you like so." Lulu held
the broom horizontal to
the floor, which was the
wrong way for sweeping
but the right way for flying.
The girls did as Lulu instructed.

"I'm going to give you a little taste of
flying." Lulu touched each one of the girls'
broomsticks as she chanted, *"Rise up. Rise
up. One centimetre, now two. Weightless and
groundless. Let the air carry you."*

Pippa gasped as the broomsticks floated in
front of them.

"Sit on your broomstick as you would sit
on a swing," Lulu continued. "Hold on and
try to stay perfectly balanced."

Trix and the other girls climbed on their besoms. The brooms floated higher and higher. It was the strangest feeling. Trix's trainers dangled in thin air. She pointed her toes to try to touch the floor, but it was now a metre below. Pippa's broom wobbled from side to side. Trix reached out to help Pippa steady herself, but instead of steadying Pippa's broom, she unbalanced her own. Trix wobbled to one side and then leaned to the other. She knocked into Pippa's broom, Pippa floated into Stella, who grabbed Cara and Becka to keep from falling, and soon five witches and five broomsticks were piled on the floor at Lulu's feet.

"Sorry," Pippa said, tears glistening in her eyes.

"It was my fault," Trix added quickly, and maybe it was, but mostly she wanted to make Pippa feel better.

"Knowing how to fall is as important as knowing how to fly," Lulu said, smiling and reaching down to help each witch to her feet. "Everyone OK?"

"My shoes got scuffed," Stella whined, rubbing at a brown patch on her pink shoes.

"Things are not as important as people," Lulu told her. "You look practically perfect to me! Tomorrow we will have our first proper flying lesson."

Trix dusted off her school uniform. She thought of how amazing it had felt to hover even a metre in the air. Then she remembered how it had felt when she'd hit the floor with a bump. *Flying wasn't as easy as it looked!*